Why Won't the Dragon Roar?

Why Won't the Dragon Roar?

By Rosalyn Rosenbluth

Drawings by Rosalie Davidson

GARRARD PUBLISHING COMPANY
CHAMPAIGN, ILLINOIS

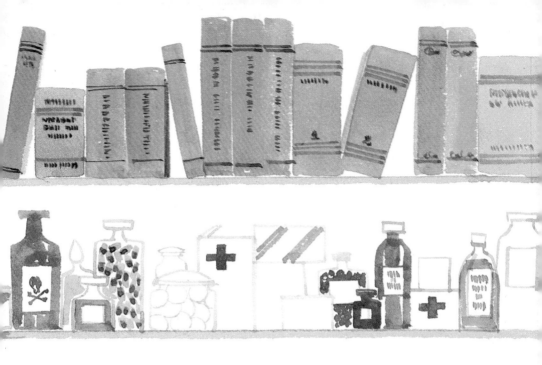

Why Won't the Dragon Roar?

Walter's mother took him
to the doctor's cave.
"What is the matter
with Walter?"
the doctor asked.

"I don't know,"
said Walter's mother.
"He does not roar.
He does not breathe fire.
He does not fight
with the other young dragons.
He likes to play with deer
and birds and rabbits."
"Hmmm," said the doctor.
"How do you feel, Walter?"
"I feel fine,"
said the young dragon.
"Open your mouth wide."
The doctor looked inside.

"Now, Walter,
let me hear you roar."
Walter opened his mouth.
But nothing came out.
"You see he does not roar,"
said Walter's mother.

"Try again," the doctor said.
Walter blew out
a tiny bit of smoke.
"Hmmm," said the doctor.
"I think I will do
a scale test.
This will only hurt a little."
Walter closed his eyes.
The doctor pulled a scale
out of Walter's tail.
He looked at it carefully.
"I can't find
anything wrong with Walter,"
the doctor said.

On the way home
Walter stopped to watch
some young dragons.
They were blowing fire
into the water.

"Come and help us,"
they called to Walter.
"Go on," said his mother.
"That's no fun," said Walter.
"I'm going home."

Soon Walter came
to his cave.
Six little rabbits
ran to him.
"Play with us, Walter,"
they called.

Walter's father came out
of the cave.
"You should be in school,"
he roared at Walter.
"I don't like school,"
said Walter.
"Go!" roared his father.

Walter walked slowly
to the school grounds.
He sat under a tree.
Each young dragon
took a turn blowing fire.

"Come be on my team, Walter,"
called his friend George.
"I don't want to,"
said Walter.
"Leave me alone."

Walter was angry
as he walked back
to his cave.
He found a big rock.
On the rock
he wrote some words.
Then he put the rock
by the cave door.
Walter smiled.
Now he felt better.
He lay down
and closed his eyes.
Suddenly he felt something
pull his tail.

Walter sat up.

It was his father!

"Get rid of that rock,"

he roared.

"Why won't you play

with the other young dragons?

The doctor says

you are not sick.

What is wrong with you?"

"There is nothing

wrong with me,"

said Walter sadly.

He did not want

his father to be angry.

He did not want
his mother to be unhappy.
But he did not want
to fight or roar
or breathe fire.
Walter went
into the forest.
The deer saw
that he was sad.
"Race us to the rocks,"
they called.
Walter was happy
as he ran with the deer
through the forest.

Soon they came
to the rocks.
There, all the young dragons
were playing fight games.
"We are going to pick
the best fighter,"
called Walter's cousin Marvin.

"Tomorrow is the battle
between the bravest knight
and the strongest dragon."
"I'm having fun
running with my friends,"
said Walter.

"I don't want to fight.
Come on!"
he called to the deer.

The next morning,
Walter's mother woke him.
"It's time to go
to the battle," she said.
"Cousin Marvin will fight
the bravest knight.
Come see who is stronger."
"I don't care who is stronger,"
said Walter.
All the other dragons
went down the mountain—
the mother dragons,
the father dragons,
and the baby dragons.

All of Walter's friends
marched down singing.
Walter was the only dragon
left on the mountain.

"Come on," he called
to the baby birds.
"I'll take you
for a ride."
The birds flew down
and sat on his tail.

"Hold on," cried Walter.
He took the little birds
for a long ride.
He jumped over big rocks.
He ran in and out
among the trees.

Suddenly something hit Walter
on his head.
He stopped.
On the ground
in front of him
was a long arrow.
"Someone is shooting at us,"
cried Walter. "Hold on!"
Walter carried
the frightened birds
back to the cave.
A deer ran up to the cave.
"Help us, Walter," she cried.
"The hunters are coming."

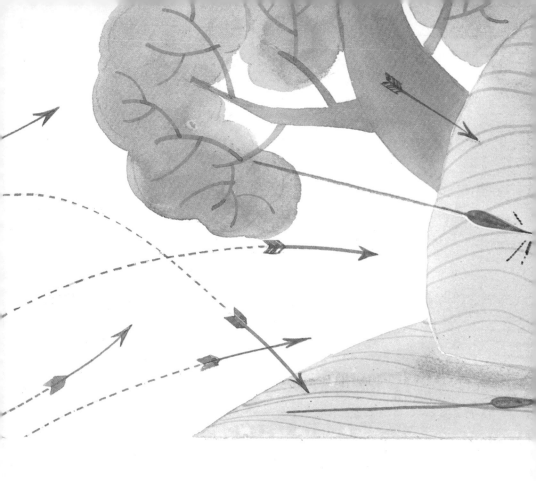

"Hide in here,"
yelled Walter. He stood
in front of the cave
to keep the arrows
from hitting his friends.

Chipmunks and rabbits
ran into the cave.
"Stay here," said Walter.
"I am going
to find the hunters."

Walter went
to the edge
of the mountain.
He could see the hunters
coming toward him.

Then one of the hunters
saw Walter standing there.
"Look!" he shouted.
"There's a dragon!
But he's not roaring
or breathing fire."

"It must be Walter,"
the others laughed.
"He won't hurt us.
And all the other dragons
are down the mountain.

We can go on hunting
the deer and rabbits."
What they said
made Walter very angry.
He walked back and forth
swinging his tail.

Now he wanted to roar
more than anything else.
He opened his mouth wide.
But no sound came out.
The hunters
were coming closer.

"Roar," cried the deer.
"Roar," called the rabbits.
"Roar," cheeped the baby birds.

Walter looked
at his frightened friends.
Suddenly
he began to feel very strange.

He started to get warm.

He got warmer and warmer.

What is happening to me?

he thought.

His mouth opened.

And then—

out came a huge roar!

"This dragon can't be Walter,"

yelled the hunters. "Run!"

"Walter has saved us!"

cried the animals.

Walter roared and roared.

He roared so loud,

the mountain shook.

He roared so loud,
the battle between Marvin
and the knight stopped.
Everyone looked up.

There stood Walter.
His head was high.
Flames were shooting
from his mouth.

At last
Walter stopped roaring.
He stopped blowing fire.
Finally he let out
one last bit of smoke.

All the dragons
hurried up the mountain.
They began to cheer.
They lifted Walter
high into the air.

"I'm so happy,"
said Walter's mother.
"Next year you will fight
the bravest knight,"
said Walter's father.
But Walter shook his head.
"No," he said.
"Fighting is not for me."

And off he ran
into the woods
with his friends.